Mr. Either/Or:
All the Rage

A Novel in Verse

Also By Aaron Poochigian

American Divine, University of Evansville Press, 2021

Mr. Either/Or, Etruscan Press, 2017

Manhattanite, Able Muse Press, 2017

The Cosmic Purr, Able Muse Press, 2012

Mr. Either/Or:
All the Rage

A Novel in Verse

Aaron Poochigian

Etruscan Press

Etruscan Press
Wilkes University
84 West South Street
Wilkes-Barre, PA 18766
(570) 408-4546

 Wilkes
University

www.etruscanpress.org

Published 2023 by Etruscan Press
Printed in the United States of America
Cover design by Logan Rock
Interior design and typesetting by Todd Espenshade
The text of this book is set in Arno Pro.

First Edition

17 18 19 20 5 4 3 2 1

Library of Congress Cataloguing-in-Publication Data

Names: Poochigian, Aaron, 1973- author.
Title: Mr. Either/Or: all the rage : a novel in verse / Aaron Poochigian.
Other titles: Mister Either/Or: all the rage
Description: First Edition. | Wilkes-Barre, PA : Etruscan Press, 2023. |
  Summary: "That mouthy and seemingly unkillable FBI agent, code name: Mr. Either/ Or, is back for more poetry and adventures! First, as a hurricane descends on New York City, he must negotiate the moods of his girlfriend Li-ling Levine while fighting to thwart militant anarchist Stavros Canard's plan to reduce humanity to chaos and violence. Will our hero fall prey to Canard's homicidal henchwoman, Aquila Blair? Will he survive learning that his girlfriend is pregnant? Barely, perhaps, because in his second adventure, retired from the Bureau and a stay-at-home husband and dad, he is sucked back in to protect a man known only as Elijah, a prophet filled with arcane Chinese wisdom about the end of the human race. As, one by one, the seven omens signaling the apocalypse come true, will our hero be able to stop the eschatological aspirations of the mad militia-leader Malachi McCann? Will he be able to sleep-train his infant daughter Savannah before Armageddon? What should you expect, reader? Imagine the bastard child of the poet Homer and Danielle Steel, imagine the rightful heir of Sappho and Lord Byron, think Hamlet in Manhattan with a license to kill"-- Provided by publisher.

Identifiers: LCCN 2022024463 | ISBN 9798985882438 (paperback)
Subjects: LCGFT: Novels.
Classification: LCC PS3616.O625 M73 2023 | DDC 813/.6--dc23
LC record available at https://lccn.loc.gov/2022024463

Please turn to the back of this book for a list of the sustaining funders of Etruscan Press.

This book is printed on recycled, acid-free paper.

Table of Contents

I.   Alfred

II.   Vision of Destruction

I. Alfred

1 "A" is for Alfred

Who is this massacre in embryo?
The sea's bad seed? The son of suck and spin?
The bastard offspring of our present rage?
Reluctant for the moment, he will grow
voraciously off Cuba. Weathermen
will name him Alfred when he comes of age.

Destined for greatness, he will carve a path
through the renowned "Graveyard of the Atlantic"
westward into our continental shelf.
How perfect that a migrant child of wrath
will lash the wrathful USA itself.
Coasts will be lost. Metropolises. Frantic
lubbers will suffer from the *mal de mer*.

See, now, the future as if CNN
were playing it before your vision, live—
a fetal revolution in the air
expanding, going category-five,
going for blood, going American.

2 Sugarbear

You woke up wanting morning sex and now
the one you love is kissing porcelain.
For four months Doc Li-Ling Levine has been
your buttercup, your minx, your scold, your Frau,
and all you wanted was some. . . was. . . *Oh, well.*
Poor woman, you can hear her retching echo
round and round inside her fancy, Deco
bathroom. What's up? (Sometimes it's hard to tell.)
You call out over the resounding din,
"Hey, honey, was it something that you ate?
The sushi maybe? Have you caught the flu?"

There is a flush, and she comes back to you
with perspiration on anemic skin
and frowzy hair afrizz and says, "I'm late."

Shuddering as the implications dawn
on you, you see your fun and freedom gone,
oodles of snot and squabbles with a shrew.

Before you can begin the dread discussion
about the stuff that might be happening
inside of her, your slick new phone goes ding.
The text reads: *Innocent-n-Naughty Russian
Nymphos Hot for a Papasha!* Whew!
The Feds have called you in. That seeming spam
means that you have an urgent rendezvous
in Chelsea Park. Director Eight, no doubt,
is there already, dying to lay out
some imminent, apocalyptic damn
monster of a maniacal attack,
and you and you alone can stop it.

                        You
are still a covert Bureau asset, still
the undergrad galoot they send to smack
sense into crooks, and break their bones, and kill.
Oh yeah, you still are Mr. Either/Or,
but you don't want to be him anymore.
The joke is old. What else could you pursue?
Phys Ed? It's like you've only got a knack
for kicking ass.
                    You turn and tell Li-ling,
"Sorry, there's somethin' that I gotta do.
Later, we'll talk about your, maybe, thing.
I mean, we've got a sweet life here. Why spoil it?"

"My thing? My thing? You have a problem, too:
Are you a killer or a daddy, Zach?
The choice is yours."
                            With that, she dashes back
into the bathroom and begins anew
to heave into her handsome, scalloped toilet.

You're off, then, Glock in pocket, dreading how
utterly life could change nine months from now.

3 Anarchy in the USA

In an immaculate flat off Verdi Square
the blond and long-haired Reverend Pete Pristine,
Faith Church's CEO and senior pastor,
is smiling, from a leather swivel chair,
at chaos on a plasma TV screen.
He sees, in the malignant mass of torque
ravaging the Atlantic, the disaster
he has been praying for—a hurricane
that will evacuate the city of New York.

This is a man whose nasal twang is heard
worldwide on Sundays as he spreads the Word.
What Word? The "gospel of material gain"—
to wit, that weekly tithing leads to health,
happiness and, what folks most covet, wealth.

Who is this holy-roller, really? Well,
underneath layers of plastic surgery,
he is a figure more aligned with Hell
than Heaven, more in tune with discord than
the Faith Church Love-choir's saccharine euphony.
It takes a very formidable man
to top the FBI's Most Wanted List
for twenty years and not get caught, and he,
Stavros Canard, malicious anarchist,
has done it.
            How he laughs when thinking of
the twist in his religious bait-and-switch:
just give your cash to me, and you'll get rich.
Money, to him, is a subservient aim
made only to promote his one great love—
chaos. His kinship with the storm is clear:
both are destructive; both are on the side

of lawlessness, but what's this madman's game?
Why does he want New York unoccupied?
What web of mischief is he weaving here?

He gives his chair a good exultant spin
then says into an intercom, "Send in
Aquila Blair."
                General Aquila Blair,
his second-in-command, the mercenary
tasked to take out irritants and bury
bodies in cement oblivion,
is good at massacres but not "all there."

In Africa, when an explosive hurled
nails at her, and she lost an eye (her right),
they fixed her up with a replacement one—
a miniature bionic sniper's sight.
Now, when she squints, she sees our precious world
through crosshairs. She can kill until the sun
goes down, then, with an emerald view at night,
keep killing till the sun comes round again.

Ah, here she comes at last! The bane of men,
the queen of mean, the hardest of the hard-
core human-hunters out there! If Canard
were capable of fear, he well might fear
her lethal look, her Ka-Bar, her disdain,
but he is not. He says,
                "Aquila dear,
the models have converged. The hurricane
I have been praying for is now en route.
Nothing can keep the last and luscious war
from starting. This time there will be no heroes
because the city will be emptied out
and ours to play with. Still, to kill all doubt,

I want you to eliminate the Bureau's
top agent, code name: Mr. Either/Or."

She smirks; she nods; she marches out the door,
sure in her heart that, when she takes men down,
she culls their power along with their renown.

4 Aquila Blair: The Origin Story

Ten years ago in Africa, before
she lost an eye and got the robot one,
Sergeant Aquila Blair—crack shot, nutjob—
had fought on our side in the shadow-war
against the mujahideen of Al-Shabaab.
That's where she met a member of the Corps,
Lieutenant Robert "Gunny" Gunnison,
who served, he said, "because this war is just."
Since she had always done these gigs for money,
she found his scruples sweet. Yes, she and Gunny
fell in love among the balsam trees
and shanty towns, among the IEDs.
She who had only ever felt disgust
with life, contempt for flesh and scorn toward men
slowly succumbed to bliss. She came to trust
he always would be there for her.
                              And then
one afternoon she saw a jet of dust
shoot up beside a field of cardamom.
Next came the blast, the smoke. A roadside bomb.
Gunny would not be meeting her again.

When morning sickness said she was with child,
what could she do but weep? At first unwilling
to let it live, she later reconciled
herself to what was in her: *No more killing.*
She would make a normal sort of home
back in her painter mother's native Rome
or with her British father in Sudan. . .

except, when she was in the caravan
bound for the next flight out, an IED
claimed her right eye, killed the pregnancy.
For years now, since her reconstruction, she

has bounced from private firm to private firm
and murdered hundreds, always wanting more
revenge, more death in retribution for
the child she never got to bring to term.

5 The Doughboy and Director Eight

For years you had been living like a poor man
with stoners in a dorm at NYU.
Now you have silk sheets, sushi and a doorman,
Massimo, to say *Good morning* to.
Life has a sheen at last, a glow, a spark.
Exulting in your new, mature, high-rent
habitat, you enter Chelsea Park
and head toward the agreed-on monument.
Of all the art that New York keeps outdoors
you love this soldier cradling his gun
the most. A doughboy slogging through a trench,
he goes on fighting, fighting World War One
(which was, they said, the war to end all wars).

You see, beside this statue, in a shady
corner, sitting on a wrought-iron bench,
what seems to be a harmless, homeless lady
digging through strollers filled with food and stuff—
Cheetos, glass bottles, last week's barbecue,
a swaddled doll and, here and there, French fries.
You sit beside her, greet her with your eyes,
and she responds with,
                               "Took you long enough."

She is, in fact, your handler in disguise,
Director Eight, who took control of you
after Director "Uh-Oh" One's demise
a few months back. An amiable shrew,
she tends to taunt you in a loving way
and so you razz her back. But not today.
Too much is happening. All urgency,
she starts right in:

"The weathermen agree:
Alfred is going to hit New York dead-on
in two days' time, this Tuesday, right at dawn.
Starting this evening, all the boroughs—Staten
Island, Bronx, Queens, Brooklyn and Manhattan—
will be evacuated. Local Bureau
personnel will move upstate until
the worst has passed, but you, our drudge, our ace,
will stay behind and mind the store in case…
who knows?
                    Our terror-level would be zero
except a steady stream of vague but shrill
chatter keeps telling us the World's Most Wanted,
Stavros Canard, has surfaced and, undaunted,
plans to strike New York. The odds of him
making a move with everything shut down
and no one left here to impress are slim.
Since you prevailed when he was last in town,
you are the natural choice."
                              Then, like the haunted
mom of a lost newborn, she lifts the doll,
gives it a kiss and chucks it on the chin,
ignoring you. (Maybe a little one
of yours is generating flawless skin
inside Li-ling. Maybe a kid is all
you need to be a man.)
                          The meeting done,
you move along, marveling at the fall
ochres and sobers and the silver sun.

The storm to end all storms is moving in.

6 Alfred in the Bahamas

Nassau had traffic lights until the wheeling
sea-beast leveled hundred-mile-per-hour
wrath at it. Now the only sort of power
is entropy. In homes along the coast
tables and chairs are knocking on the ceiling;
reef sharks are in the kitchens. Families
are clinging to the rooftops, to the trees
and flagpoles, to each other. Outermost
New Providence has gone to join Atlantis.

On Musha Kay a priest is saying, *Grant us,
O Lord, your peace,* while at upscale resorts
tourists are not enjoying water sports
now that the ocean is inside their rooms.
Many of them will not go home undrowned.
Many of them will not even be found.

Much that is dry, O Lord, will soon be wet.
Much that is tranquil soon will thrill to Doom's
toccata.
     Alfred is a young storm yet.

7 The Master Key

A good mile south of you, where Varick Street
meets Houston, there are bollards and a very
tight-lipped office-building that contains
Homeland Security's new subsidiary,
Cyber Defense. Its purpose: to defeat
everything from election-meddling
to hacker blitzkriegs on the banking sector.
A special vetted corps of total brains
works here at all hours under the command
of SA Michael Sanger, the director
of this new branch's speculative wing.

Sanger is now, like many times before,
standing inside a foyer with his hand
flat on a sensor so that it can check
his fingerprints against a file ID.
He is approved. Proprietary-tech
gadgetry disengages, and a door
unseals itself and opens, and he strides
into a laboratory whose insides
are spare: a desk, a chair, and a PC.
The room is specially designed to host
his toy, The Master Key.
                              "The Master Key?"
Software that tracks a given online post
back to its source and instantly provides
a target's actual name and aliases,
current location (based upon his phone),
playlists, associates, home and work addresses,
and passwords for his personal accounts.
The military, then, can choose to pounce
with a precision airstrike from a drone
or just sit back and monitor, unseen,
his virtual and real-world whereabouts.

Sanger, the maker of the "Key," had doubts
at first: What if a hacker found a hole in
their best defenses? What if it were stolen?
That's why it dwells inside a lone machine
kept disconnected from the Internet.
It is, at times, hooked up to do a hack
and then most expeditiously put back
in solitary. There's too great a threat
the Russians, maybe, or Assange might get
ahold of it.
                    He hooks up the computer,
cracks his knuckles and begins to track
messages from an Al-Shabaab recruiter
through a Yemeni-masked Somali server
to fixed coordinates. The fellow's fervor
and afterlife must have enticed enough
boys to the cause to make the Brass get rough.
But that's not Sanger's business. He's a nerd.
He taps a final "Enter" on the keyboard
and then unplugs the thing.
                                A hurricane
is heading north along the Eastern Seaboard—
that is at least the news that he has heard
third-hand from coworkers. He will remain
to mind the tech toys while the storm blows through,
but he expects he won't have much to do.

8 Malignant Dread

Why this malignant dread? This freak-attack?
Yes, just like that, while you are walking back
to 7th Ave to catch a train downtown
to get in hours, maybe, of drinking time
or something and avoid Li-ling, it's like
all of creation wants to drop a dime
on you, like everybody has a mic
or pinhole camera. What about that clown
with wild mustachios? Or maybe her
rocking the lace and kohl, the vamp voyeur?
They all just freak you out as you go down
the stairwell to the subway. You have learned
to trust these sinking feelings; you have earned
the right to be completely paranoid.

Miffed, in a way, to find the platform void
of superspies, or anyone at all,
you sigh impatiently. You shrug. You pace.
You can't help reaching down to touch your gun
just to be sure it's waiting, just in case.

What noise is on the stairs? Footsteps and voices
echo like music in a music hall.
They say that life depends on choices, choices.
The violent things we do can't be undone.
You can't just shoot because of a suspicion
'cause then you would be offing everyone.

Four guys come round the bend in white shirts, ties
and black dress-pants like Mormons on a mission.
And are those bulges in their pockets? What,
pistols or rolled-up Holy Writ? Your gut
insists these dudes are killers in disguise.

All smiles and meekness, coming close to you,
the tallest asks *Is this the northbound track?*
Up to The Cloisters?
                         What you gonna do?
Offer directions? Run away? Fight back
preemptively?
                         Oh no, you see his hand
reach for his pocket; you start reaching, too.
He comes up with a snub nose Ruger, and. . .

9 Dude, Are You Dead?

You blow his brains out.
                    Brother Whatever
flaps and flops
                flat on the platform,
and you run up the rails,
                    the rat-road, to darkness
with impious utterances,
                pistol-replies,
whizzing around you.

                  Way back among
the pitch-smutched posts
                  that part the express
from the local line,
            you look toward the station:
the three still standing
                  are standing there staring
at what must be merely
                murk to their eyes.
A fourth joins them,
              a female rocking
dark fatigues.
            She tells the men off,
orders them after you.
                They all jump down.

Left-eye asquint,
              she seems somehow
to draw a bead
             through the dust and darkness.
Instantly a Heckler
            is in her hand,
and bullets bite

the beam that hides you,
graze your hair.
That harpy can discern
game in the gloom!
What a gifted killer!

You, death-dodger,
dance in and out
among the trusses,
move till you find
a concrete barrier
to crouch behind.
The shots stop,
but stone starts shaking:
the 1 is coming,
a worm on wheels.

Your foes, it seems,
have formed a scheme—
they rush you firing
round after round
to force you from
your defensive position.
That's a lot of lead!
Dislodged, you can only
retreat up the tracks.
The train is right there
honk-honk-honking,
its headlights blinding. . .

Dude, are you dead?
Doh! You escaped
by leaping over
to a little ledge
next to the tracks.

You were not quite another
train-tragedy.
They tried like Hell
to do you in,
but you didn't die.
It's time for you, prey,
to turn predator.

10 The Gospel of Prosperity

Here in a shaft, with rungs beneath your feet,
you are the very model of persistence.
Still living, you are tracking, at a distance,
your failed antagonists. You climb, climb, wait
till they have finished wrestling with a grate,
then make your way out, too. Back on the street
you watch the four of them approach, on 8th,
a white building as tall as Lincoln Center.
There is an iron cross out front, the perch
of many inner-city doves of faith.
What do your would-be killers want at church?

It's Sunday morning, and you see them enter
the sacred space with flocks of faithful—some
decked out in suits and dresses, some in jeans
and concert tees. Well, since it seems that all
are welcome, in you go.
                              The entrance hall
opens into a sort of stadium
with rows on rows of theater seats for pews.
Everywhere super-jumbo TV screens
live-stream the members of a Christian band
crooning in chorus from a focal stage:

Who, when stocks crash on the Day of Rage,
will still be wealthy in the Promised Land?
Riches are coming! Have you heard the news?
Riches are coming! Have you paid your dues?

Worshippers like antennas of the Lord
receive the power of each power-chord
with open arms.

Flash!, then: a smoke-machine
discharges frankincense into the air;
the band fades; and a man with long blond hair
appears on stage, appears on every screen,
in denim and a studded leather jacket.
With a Kentucky twang of boundless love,
he says,
   "I am the Reverend Pete Pristine
and, friends, I have some awesome news to share,
a cause for jubilation: God above
wants you to join a higher income-bracket."

. . . . .

"Christians, this Sunday's sermon will concern
frustration, tithing and prosperity.
Its title: *We Must Give So We Can Earn.*

One day a non-believer said to me:
'Life's hard. I get up every day at dawn
and work, work, work and still don't get ahead.'
Well, I took pity on the man. I said,
'Have faith and, if you pay God what is due
to God, He will be there enriching you
every day in every way.'
     In *John*
the Savior says, *I'm come that they might live
with greater plenitude.* In *Malachi*
the Lord Omnipotent pronounces, *Give
to me a tenth of what you earn. . . and I
shall open heaven's windows for your sake
and pour out all the blessings you desire.*
(Such richness flows from ol' Hebrew and Greek.)

The man I met was smart enough to take
advice, and now, believers, he's on fire—

buying up islands, serving on the board
of GE, all because he gave the Lord
a tenth of what he took in every week.
It's no hard principle for folks to learn:
a person has to give so he can earn."

The Reverend goes on citing evidence
connecting offerings to affluence,
then guides the faithful through collective prayer:
he tells them to be silently confessing
not doubts or sins (that's for the church of Rome)
but some particular material blessing
they really want—a new car, a new home.
If they do this while waving in the air
a donative of ten percent or more
(and give the sum with true humility),
no matter who they might be, rich or poor,
the blessing they desire will come to be
as surely as the Lord will come again
some day to claim the worthiest of men.

". . . Why do we pay? For something in return.
A person has to give so he can earn."

So ends the Reverend, and the band starts playing
electric gospel, and the crowd is swaying,
and you are swaying, too. American,
is this the wisdom, this the system that
will make you in the Valley of Jehoshaphat?

11 Temporal Affairs

Time to return to temporal affairs.
The faithful heading for the exit doors,
you push against the streetward movement, slowly,
smilingly working toward a set of stairs.
Why not go poke about the private floors
in search of God knows what: Dry bones? The holy
of holies? Why a gang of the devout
hunted you down and tried to take you out?

After you make your way down several levels,
the tramp of feet says you've got company.
You duck back up but peek in time to see
more of those white-shirt fellows, handsome devils,
march past. They have a military feel,
like Templars, maybe, or the Pope's Swiss Guard.
Are they the real deal or a pious fraud?
Are you the Archfiend that these 'men of God'
came after you? They should have left you be.

You tip-toe down a hall and reach a steel
door, that is locked, but slant-bolt locks aren't hard.
Swiping your plastic college ID Card
between the latch and frame, you laugh, then enter
darkness and chilled air and the muted heat
of pent-up megawatts and gigabytes.
The echoes emanating from your feet
suggest a vasty room. A Data Center?

You grope the wall until you find the lights,
then blink and squint at hardware, tower by tower,
row on row, like stacks in some neglected
library annex. You can feel the floor
abuzz like wasps; the very airwaves, humming.

Whoever plugs in here would be connected
to one mean stockpile of computing power.
What does a church need Google wattage for?

More footsteps in the hallway—someone's coming.
Retreating on the instant several rows
into the server farm, you hear the door
open. A sacrilegious basso goes,

"Come on, surrender, and we will forgive
your trespasses. Come out, and you will live."

12 Godzilla

Why wait? These white-shirts
                              won't just vanish.
To Hell with it: Glock-Nine
                              held overhead,
you pop off replies,
                              and pillars of components,
wired spires,
                              explode in sparks.
Loath to harm
                    the high-tech hardware,
the parish foot-soldiers
                              refuse to fire back,
stalk you instead.
                    Stacks of servers
cover their coming.
                    Clever bastards,
they will try tackling you,
                              a team effort.

Ah, but the rocking
                    of the rack-mounted routers
gives you, Eureka!,
                              a grand idea:
Why shoot your gun
                    when your shoulder will do?
You charge and topple
                    some techno-totems,
which knock over
                    their nearest neighbors—
and so on, like dominoes,
                              the data dolmens
fall and, in falling,
                    fell each other.

A chain-reaction!
                    Cheered by the sound
of zap and crash,
                      you exult like Godzilla
destroying toy
                    towers in Tokyo.
What a spectacle!
                    The spreading collapse
has crushed, you hope,
                        the crouching hostiles,
rubbed them out.

                  You run at random
through the remaining
                      maze of modules
and, at the far end,
                    find a fire-door.
It opens outward;
                  all is clear.

Hot to get
            the Hell out now,
you mount the stairs
                    that meet you, leaping.
Four flights up,
                you find, on the floor
with the spacious nave,
                    no one at first
to shun or shoot
                but, *Shit*, then, *Oof*,
you run into someone
                    rounding a corner—
the darkness-markswoman,
                    that mean mother
who hunted you before.

The head-on impact
loosens your grip,
        and your Glock goes flying.
Before she can point
        her piece your way
and pump your guts,
        you grab her gun-hand
and make her loose
        her load of lead
into the ceiling.
        A savage knee
below your belt,
        and she breaks the hold.

Quick as breath,
        her Ka-bar comes out,
and there's no way round her
        to reach the street.
Whoosh, whoosh, slicing
        wind from the air
to flaunt her knife-craft,
        she announces, sneering:
"I've wanted to kill you
        for quite some time—
the golden boy,
        the Bureau's best."

Who is this chick
        that hates you so?

She feints, feints, lunges
        and, lumbering palooka,
you bob and weave
        the best you can,
death-dancing.
        Damn, she's slick.

Biding time
            until the psycho
goes, finally,
            too far with a slash,
you snatch and wrench
                her wrist with your right hand
and with your left
            deliver no lightweight
hook to her temple.
                She topples quick.
Still worked up,
            you start strangling her,
but the resonant tramp
                of troops intrudes
before you're through.
                Freeing her throat,
you collect your Glock
                and leave at last
that homicidal
            house of faith.

13 Too Much To Face

What with a pack of wackos trying (twice)
to take you out this morning, you are pretty
hungry, so you have gone to get a slice
at Ed's on 8th. The tile beneath your shoes
is slick with grease, the silverware is gritty—
a poor man's sort of hospitality.

A TV on the wall has got the news:
the governor is up in Albany
saying the storm of storms will make landfall
Tuesday at dawn. The whole of New York City
will be evacuated starting Sunday
(today) at 1pm. Tomorrow (Monday),
they will complete the work of shutting down
the subway. Barring first responders, all
Gothamites should be getting out of town
ASAP by car, bus, train, or plane.
DO NOT, he says, ride out this hurricane.
The winds will reach 200 miles per hour.
Storm surge predicted, frequent lightning, rain
and, for a week or more, as aftermath,
Biblical flooding, widespread loss of power.

Oh well, you think, while shaking Parmesan
onto a wedge of Sausage-and-Gruyère,
*after this morning, you could use the bath
and weeks off-grid.*
               With all that's going on,
you want to sneak off somewhere, anywhere
outside the world a while and just not care. . .

What will this monster Alfred not destroy?
Why were assassins sent to snuff you out?

Oh God, is Li-ling pregnant? Girl or boy?
Too much to think about, too much to face. . .

Eight hours in O'Sullivan's Saloon
milking disaster from the Cow of Doubt,
and you somehow, a drunken stumbling goon,
have stumbled through the frantic, wall-to-wall
evacuation back to Li-ling's place.
You are in trouble: you ignored her call.

Neon in Chelsea and a cloud-strained moon
light, through her bedroom window, wads of tissue
along the carpet, on her comforter,
and there she lies, all legs and camisole.
You want to go to her; you know you should
but just can't move to do it.
                                If you were
a better man, this wouldn't be an issue.
You would duly climb in next to her,
embrace her waist and pray for fatherhood.
As it is, diffident, you need some distance
to ponder what might be a wee existence
down in there, in her little Possum pouch.

Who knows, man? Maybe you would be as good
at changing diapers as you are at, well,
snipering members of a drug cartel,
lying, defusing bombs or
                                . . . blitzed as Hell,
you weep awhile, then pass out on the couch.

(But she is only faking being sunk
in slumber. She can feel the hurricane
inside of you; she knows the covert pain
of your profession, your distress, your sorrow.

It's no use talking to a maudlin drunk.

Best let you sleep. She'll try again tomorrow.)

14 Alfred Off Cape Hatteras

While you are snoring up a storm, your mouth
ajar and drooling in the hours toward dawn,
a real and raucous storm is going on
east of Manhattan and a short flight south
in the renowned "Graveyard of the Atlantic."

Brisk as a race car, giddy, Corybantic,
its central swirl is scattering the doubloons
of pirate troves across the ocean floor.
Already arms of it have swung ashore
at lonesome Cape Hatteras, breached the dunes
and turned the choicest real estate to water.

Wake up! Wake up! There is a squall as wide
as Texas coming for you!
                            On you snore,
dreaming your hands are out to catch a daughter
descending, squealing, a tornado slide.

15 Tater Tots

You are the hero, yes, but, sleepy-head,
since you are dozing through the morning, we
will leave you, fly to Soho and instead
observe Mike Sanger, who has stepped outside
the office of Homeland Security
to hunt for food to make it through the storm.

The clouds, the clouds, like ghost-ships in the sky,
have made even the stubborn run and hide.
There are no cabs, no vendors, just a swarm
of crows. Where is that crazy homeless guy,
the King of King St, with his paper cup
for change, spare change?
                              At Sonny's Super Mart
(the only place not closed and boarded up)
the special agent fills his squeaky cart
with Pizza Pockets, nuggets, Tater tots
and finally, to make the binge complete,
two tubs of "Triple Chocolate Birthday Cake"
ice-cream.
                  It's all banal until, surprise,
when he is back out on the empty street
just walking, whistling, thinking his own thoughts,
he hears tires squeal behind his back and brake
shrilly. He turns and stares as clean-cut guys
in black suit pants and white dress-shirts and ties
leap from a van and trap him in a ring.
Oof, then, a gut-punch knocks the breath out of him.
Poor Michael Sanger! When they lift and shove him
into a backseat, he can only sputter,
"Wha'?" And the groceries he was carrying
are left defrosting in the flooded gutter.

16 Human Chorionic Gonadotropin (hCG)

Late morning. You are talking to Li-ling.
Well, she is talking. You are listening.
She won't stop using that detached, ungentle,
hyper-factual tone of hers:
                              "...You see,
there would be a detectable placental
effluvium, the hormone hCG,
issuing from the, maybe, embryo
lodged in the lining of my uterus..."

You cut in,
            "Whoa. Hey, call me sentimental,
but kill the hormone-talk. Just say you pee
on something and it answers *Yes* or *No*.
Alert me if there's business to discuss,
and we'll debate the, well, you know, the 'It.'"

"Alright, if I can find a store still open
in spite of Alfred, I will buy a kit
and test my urine for Gonadotropin."

"Great. Then I'll help you catch a shuttle bus
to Scranton, maybe, or somewhere upstate.
(But, hey, like, call me right away if you
are preg, and we'll talk over what to do.)"

That should have settled it—except Li-ling
insists that she will not evacuate
like everybody else who has a brain.
She is, of course, in charge of conservation
for the Met Museum's Asian wing,
and she will spend the whole damn hurricane
just making sure her art does not get wet.

Yep, you have lost this fight. For all the threat
of flood and gale and utter devastation,
Li-ling (who may be carrying your child)
will stay in town. Just great. You will have her
to worry over when the wind goes wild.
O life was so much simpler when you were
a free-and-easy loser bachelor.

17 The Age of Anger

There had been kicks and punches; there had been
a blackout, then vague pain. Now that the daze
has lifted, Michael Sanger can appraise
the helpless situation he is in:
he has been duct-taped to a wooden chair
in what looks like a church refectory.
He sees doughnuts and dainty cups for tea.
His shoes are gone, and someone big is there—
one of the "missionaries" standing guard
beside him with unanimated eyes.

Eventually a guy with long blond hair
enters and cracks a joke:
                    "No, please don't rise.
I am, and pardon the absurd disguise,
the man, the myth, the real Stavros Canard,
and I am fortunate: I have a grand
design. Believe me, you will lend a hand
to help me realize it, Agent Sanger.
Sit back, now. Listen closely. Understand.

I love this age, my age, the Age of Anger.
I love the Internet, the vitriol
of Red on Blue and troll attacking troll.
That's where I feel it: we are on the verge
of something great. Thus far the privacy
of passwords and the anonymity
of usernames have—damn them all!—impeded
the luscious violence aching to emerge.

That is where you come in. Your 'Master Key'
is just the miracle that we have needed
to put us at each other's fingertips
and, thus, each other's throats. Yes, when I share

your well-meant code with everyone out there,
I will at last get the apocalypse
I've longed for—rage and riot, tar
and feathers.
              Just imagine: if you are
the victim of a personal attack
on Twitter, you will have the power to track
the bastard down and go and kick his ass
or drain his bank accounts and, just for laughs,
email the press his pervy photographs.
Yes, all our online insults, all our crass
bullying soon will blossom into action.
Party will punish party; faction, faction.
Old friendships will explode. Ah, ha, ha, ha!
No inhibitions, no lame rule of law,
only a luscious pandemonium!
A scrum deluxe! A cataclysmic rout!
I dote on the disgrace we will become.

Tomorrow, when the town is emptied out
because of Alfred, I will lead a band
of soldiers to Homeland Security,
where, with the kind assistance of your hand
(but not your body, not your chest or arms),
I will at last obtain The Master Key.
Then I will use my many server farms
to make this tool available for free
to everybody on the Internet,
and all our malice, every hearth-felt threat,
will boil over into reality.

Don't do it, Sanger—don't call me insane.
No, I am merely wickeder-than-thou.
Why am I saying this? A hurricane
grows great on sultry air; I thrive on fear.
I needed you alive, my friend, to hear

my plot, to feed me terror through your eyes.
Thank you for that, but I am sated now,
and what comes next should come as no surprise."

Sanger has started struggling to get loose
and begging for his life: "Christ Jesus, Wait!
What if you need me? I could operate
the Master Key for you!"
                    (No use. No use.)

The madman nods, and the attendant thug
moves in behind the agent, grabs his throat
and squeezes.
            It's like being on a drug,
they say, the way awareness starts to float
above the skull and gather on the ceiling.
They say it is a special sort of feeling.

18 ID Unknown

Already what will be a real rager
is offering hors d'oeuvres—relentless rains
and bouts of bluster. All the subway trains
are sleeping now, so you are slogging down
to NYU to talk to "Woot" McGraw,
pot-smoker and Computer Science Major.
He chose, as "Lord Warcraft," to stay in town
and face the consequences of the storm—
the floods, dead fish, and days of martial law—
rather than leave the console in his dorm.

When you describe the server farm you saw
at Faith Church, Inc., he snorts and answers,
                                        "Uh,
giants like Microsoft, of course, have vast
centers like that out in, like, Iowa,
but stacks of servers 'stretching row on row
forever' in Manhattan? I don't know.
Real estate's too damn pricey. Furthermore,
why would a church have secretly amassed
all that bandwidth, all that download speed?

But, hey, let's say you really saw it. Fine.
Bad guys might use that sort of wattage for
dark-web activities, you know—online
drug-trafficking, child-trafficking, live-feed
porno, machine-gun dealerships, whatever,
or someone who was really, really clever
could lie low, then just burst onto the scene
and take the web by storm. . ."
                              Ring, ring, your phone,
ring, ring, is butting in. You check the screen,
but Caller ID says "ID Unknown."

"Hello?"
           A purposeful contralto purrs,
"Listen: I've got your would-be wifey wife
at gunpoint at your flat. Checkmate. You're done.
Let's do a quid pro quo—your hide for hers.
Be here in twenty minutes. Come alone."

"Who's this?"
                The voice replies,
                           "I am the one
that nearly cut your nuts off with my knife,
the one that nicked you with my Heckler. Friend,
I am your destiny. I am The End."

The voice is gone. Your buddy Woot has grown
blurry beside you, and you start to run
not for your own but for your lover's life.

19 Desolation

No cabs to take,
                no cars to jack—
and so, adrenal
                in the driving rain,
you are running north
                to the rescue, stud.
Fast as you are, though,
                you feel defeat
hard on your heels.
                That harpy threatening
Li-ling's life
                won't let her keep it;
you've gotta go
                and give yours, anyway,
die, too, for your darling.

                Desolation!
No gull is here
                to gape at you going
through old Manhattan
                all alone,
no Norway rat
                to note the splat
of soggy Converses
                on soaked sidewalks
and flooded streets.

                The Strand Book Store
bobs by on your right
                with boards on its windows
and soon, to your left,
                lights-out and shuttered,
Chase Bank and Brenner's
                Chocolate Bar.

General Washington,
               who won his war,
is sitting in stirrups
               astride a steed
in Union Square,
               while you, a young
campaigner of note,
               a promising patriot,
must face on foot
               a final failure.

Guilt (what you've gotten
               your girlfriend into!)
wells up on Broadway
               near the Brooks Brothers.
By the time you turn
               on Twenty-Eighth,
you want what's coming,
               wicked one.

20 That Woman

All, all alone: no doorman standing sentry,
no gaudy matrons waiting in the entry,
no human ear to which you can confide
your odds of dying on the seventh floor.
You press the button for the elevator
urgently and, what feels like eons later,
a little bell rings, and you step inside.
After a slow agony of a ride,
you burst into the hall and see the door
to Li-ling's flat is open.
                              Pistol drawn,
you enter, scowling, find the living room
empty, the kitchen empty. Gliding on
past the solarium and bathroom, past
the study with its Japanese wood-block
print of a storm at sea, you find at last
that woman, the embodiment of Doom,
sneering while standing in the bedroom, gun
aimed at the tummy of your bathrobed one-
and-only, Doc Li-ling Levine.
                              The shock
is just too much for you. You drop your piece
and tell the hag,
                    "Here I am, now release
my girlfriend—that's the deal."
                              And then the Doc
starts crying:
              "Zach, I really need to live.
The test I took today was positive!"

21 Family Matters

Here is what happens after Li-ling's plea:

on learning of the little hurricane
inside your lover's womb, your enemy,
though she had got you beat, though she had won,
shudders and swings the muzzle of her gun
away from Li-ling's stomach. This humane
gesture of deference to pregnancy
provides you with the perfect opening:

dying to off the crone and save the day,
you dive at her and knock her gun away.
Although she starts out under you, she twists
sideways and flips around and lands astraddle
your torso. Both arms pinned, you cannot fling
the homicidal jockey from the saddle.
Reveling in her power as her fists
pummel your face, she whoops and giggles, then
pausing just long enough to draw her knife,
ululates, as she does when stabbing men.
She would have killed you if your would-be wife
had not crept up and brained her with a lamp.

The stunned witch pauses, and you grab her hand,
invert the blade and push it through her heart.
The sneer forsakes her lips, her green eyes start,
and all at once her camo shirt grows damp.
Killing is never glorious, never grand,
just ugly, but that homicidal vamp
threatened your girl, your child, your everything.

Pushing the body off your chest, you stand
and hug your lover, smiling from a mug
hot with abrasions. Though your kisses sting

your lips, who cares? You have a family—
you, and the little one, and sweet Li-ling.
That nightmare creature on the Persian rug,
whoever she had been, has ceased to be.

22 One Plus One Is Three

You can relax now, killer. You have rolled
the monster's corpse up in the blood-stained rug
and dumped the whole burrito in a cold
puddle behind Armando's Midtown Deli.
It could be weeks before the thing gets found.

Yes, you have done your chores and now are snug
in bed and fondling Li-ling's little belly,
imagining the kid inside of her
in black and white, like in an Ultrasound.

(The "we" you are has now increased to three.)

Mostly asleep, you mumble,
                              "If I were
to get a ring, what size should it, like, be?

"Was that, like, a proposal?"
                              "Yeah, I guess."

She laughs, then answers you: a cosmic "Yes."

(Afterward, though, in an exhausted silence
all the nasty things you have to do
for work descend on her. She lies there seeing
criminal menaces, vile acts of violence.
How could she not half regret agreeing
to take your name and raise a child with you?)

. . . . .

The wind is full disquiet, and the rain
raucous percussion on the windowpane,
and you are grateful. You are good and warm

and glad your girlfriend didn't go upstate
and leave you desolate for, God knows, weeks.
You love the heat of her; you love the storm.

And then your phone rings. It's Director Eight.
She starts right in with,
                              "Listen. We've got trouble.
Michael Sanger, keeper of the geeks
at DHS in Soho, disappeared
six hours ago. What if the worst we feared
has come to pass? What if Stavros Canard
is back?
            I want you down there on the double,
first, making sure all's well, then, standing guard
over this software called 'The Master Key.'
It's classified; it has priority.
Now go."
            And so you leave the comfortable
nest where your love lies with your son or daughter
safe in amnion and Charmeuse sheets.
Outside, the gusts are madness, and the streets
vanishing under mad amounts of water.

23 Alfred in Manhattan

High up Manhattan climbs the angry sea.
Good bye, South Ferry; good bye, Battery.
The Harbor House has foundered; the whole Park
joined the dominion of the squid and shark.
Futures are bad, the Dow is going down,
while someone's sloop—or is it Noah's Ark?—
without a helmsman, without flag or sails,
is bobbing up Canal in Chinatown.

The trees that stand are writhing in the gales.
Bicycles, chairs, trashcans and signage, all
loose things, lift off and wheel into a wall
or spin away into the troposphere.

If Anarchy is Hell, then Hell is here.

24 What Must Be

God damn this storm! you think as, itty-bitty
beneath its magnitude, you slog down 8th.
No signs of life. You are a lonesome wraith
haunting what once had been a vibrant city.
The task your boss has set you seems so dumb.
Really, what act of evil could be done
this sodden morning during Kingdom Come?
Who else would brave this mess?
                          In fact, while you
are splatting onward underneath no sun
at dawn, the anarchist Stavros Canard
is riding shotgun down 9th Avenue,
a convoy at his back. Since everyone
has run for high ground, and the National Guard
has yet to move in, all New York is his—
his and his 'missionary mercenaries'—
to loot and play with. The bloody hand he carries
used to belong to a computer wiz
named Michael Sanger. Now, hacked off, it is
Canard's great hope of capturing The Key.

Inexorably, as insane waves drown
the margins of Manhattan, you and he
are heading south, south to the same downtown
Department of Homeland Security.

25 Regarding What You Do

Alfred has nothing on the heaving brew
of angst you are. Walloped internally,
you founder, and your mind goes melancholic:

What will you do with this absurdity,
this livelihood that won't stop killing you?
It's like, God damn, for all your special talents,
you've blown it: an aspiring alcoholic,
you dote on guns and violence; you're a jerk;
you hate yourself.
                  Regarding what you do,
there is, of course, no way of "finding balance."
Your job refuses to be nine-to-five.
Trouble will come and catch you sleeping; work
will spill over and drown your child and wife.
You should be not just keeping them alive
but giving them a safe, like, Rockwell life.

Your saner voices keep repeating, *Stop
the madness. Go and be a rent-a-cop
somewhere, doze through your shifts and come home chubby
for dinner. O go be the perfect hubby,
set out each morning with a goodbye kiss
and spend your weekends lounging in the yard.*

Alright, then: you'll reject the interference
keeping you from the heights of happiness.
You'll do this stupid "farewell" job, find out
for sure the cause of Sanger's disappearance
is really (duh) that fiend Stavros Canard.
Soon as you slay him, you'll be done for good.
Then bring on marriage; bring on fatherhood.
A private coup d'état will come about!

Risen from your own swirling depths, you shout
into the storm, "Soon, soon, I will be free
to revel in complete normality!"

26 What She Expects Now that She's Expecting

Sound waves will plumb me, then the doctor's glove,
rummaging, then the wonder will emerge—
the thick head slow, the body quick and slim.
Where is the father? A maternal urge
darkens my thinking when I think of him:
Sometimes we cannot keep the ones we love.

Cloaks, daggers—that's what I am frightened of.
Clearly from now on what I need to do
is shield this smidge of life the best I can.
Zach ran to save us (and he saved us, too)
but he is much too hazardous a man.
Sometimes we cannot keep the ones we love.

Zach, a grunt with orders from above,
will always need to put his country first.
There will be terror on a plane, train, bus—
I know for certain worse will come to worst,
and he will choose disaster over us.
Sometimes we cannot keep the ones we love.

Oh, in my ninth month, push will come to shove,
but where will Zach be when the time arrives?
What if I call, and he ignores his phone?
Because of him I almost lost two lives
today, this tadpole future's and my own.
Sometimes we cannot keep the ones we love.

27 Kaboom!

Soon as you shove your Bureau ID Card
against the plexiglass, the door goes buzz.
Inside, you smile and feel annoyed because
there is no crisis, no Stavros Canard,
only Miguel DeVera, junior coder
and Heather Hackenrude, his supervisor,
and cubicles and the distinctive odor
of burnt coffee.
              Miguel is quiet; Heather
(pant-suited, belted with a golden chain),
chatty:
        "How about this crazy weather?
Either you are a very early riser
and just love hiking in the wind and rain
or something serious is up. What is it
that brought you out to us?"
              When you explain
that you were told to come and pay a visit
because of Michael Sanger's disappearance,
Heather says,
        "I hardly know the guy,
but, with the storm, there's lots of reasons why
he might be AWOL."
             When you ask to see
the backroom where they keep The Master Key,
she answers,
        "Sorry, but we don't have clearance.
No one, and I mean NO ONE, sees that vault
except the chosen few who wear the right
fingerprints. No method of assault—
machine-gun fire, bazooka shell, C-4—
is getting through that reinforced steel door.
Trust me, The Master Key is locked up tight

in there, and nobody, including you,
will visit it today."
                    As if on cue,
Kaboom!, a big loud blast. The streetside wall
explodes and tumbles toward you. Rubble buries
Miguel the quiet programmer, and all
Alfred comes howling in. The sudden squall,
blowing the smoke away, reveals Lord knows
how many hostiles dressed like missionaries
leaping through the blasthole, gun in hand.
Goddammit, you will have to make a stand,
you and the chick, against a mess of foes.

28 Remember the Alamo

You get your gun out
                        and go nuts shooting
one intruder,
                two of them, ten,
but more move in,
                        their Mac 10s spraying
the room at random.
                        Routed, you take
cover behind
                a cabinet on casters—
risible redoubt.
                        Barrages riddle
its drawers, the dry wall,
                        the drop ceiling.
What can you do
                but duck and cuss?

You see, five feet
                from your frail bastion,
Heather the sassy
                supervisor
holding her own
                behind a desk.
Pistol drawn,
                she is pop-pop-popping
the unwelcome white-shirts,
                        one by one.
Braver than you,
                she breaks her cover,
rushes the marauders.
                        A rash move:
machine-guns shred
                her shirt and person.

(Noble woman,
　　　　　　you went down fighting.
You live now forever
　　　　　　in literature.)

The swarm as one
　　　　　　then swings its attention
back your way.
　　　　　　Bullets bite
cubicle and copier,
　　　　　　a coffee maker.
Fluorescent fixtures
　　　　　　rock and sputter
above your head.
　　　　　　You hear the creak
of fraying tension,
　　　　　　and rectangular tiles
come raining down,
　　　　　　the runners with them.
The viperous length
　　　　　　of a vent collapses.
You get brained and buried.
　　　　　　The barbarian horde
shushes its machine-guns,
　　　　　　sure, it seems,
the avalanche killed you.

　　　　　　Ever the survivor,
you lie pinned
　　　　　　in a pile of rubble,
woozily watching
　　　　　　what is apparently
the shepherd of all
　　　　　　this shock and awe
(a longhair, lean,
　　　　　　with celebrity skin)

make his way
                among the commandos,
holding a, no,
                a hacked-off hand?
It must have come
                from the kidnapped coder,
Michael Sanger.
                The suave savage
puts the meat
                palm-down on a scanner,
presses the five
                fingers flat
beneath his own.

                Now you get it:
that severed hand
                and Hurricane Alfred
unpeopling the streets
                were parts of a plot
to crack a vault
                and carry off
The Master Key.

                Motorized bolts
unlock a door
                that leads to Lord knows
what sort of weapon
                is waiting in there.
The psycho goes in,
                soon emerges
flush with victory.
                Flash drive in hand,
he parades back out
                through the ruptured wall
with all his mercs
                marching behind him.

Coughing, cursing,
                     kicking, writhing,
you rise from the wreckage,
                          raw, vengeful
and alive at least
                a little longer.

29 The Lord of Misrule

Let's turn, now, to the happiest man on earth:

the least removed that he has been since birth
from perfect bliss, Stavros Canard admires
trees that have toppled from the boulevard
and dropped on cars, storefronts and upper stories.
He giggles through a windshield at live wires
writhing and smashed glass (every poignant shard)
and sodden lumps of vermin and the glories
of mud on streets and promising young fires
in high-rent towers. Such joy he feels, such joy
on this the morning of his great success.

Like any child, he loved to make a mess.
Hyper at choir practice, he would sing
off-pitch on purpose. He dismembered toy
heroes while cackling in ecstasy.
Still, he was just a naughty little boy,
a brat, a nuisance. He was not yet "strange."
Then came his sexual awakening:
one day, alone, he felt intense arousal
while watching a tsunami on TV.
Then Stavros hankered to do more than tousle
a playmate's well-combed hair and disarrange
the volumes in the public library.

So he began his villainous career
fomenting anarchy in gay Par-ee,
had triumphs and defeats year after year,
and then this morning: like a hedonist
anticipating, just before a tryst,
a gonzo Eden of ecstatic sex,
he revels in the prospect of a welter

of ruinous dystopian effects
reducing humankind to free-for-all
in-fighting, feud and famine, Helter-Skelter—
that is the world he itches to be in.

He is the cure; he is the wrecking ball.
He is the happiest that he has ever been.

30 The Cone of Shine

Outside the breach
           blown in the building
you meet a marvelous
             morning inside
cyclonic cloud,
        a cone of shine.
The eye is on you,
        an eerie clarity
moving inland.

        Though most of the motorcade
has headed north,
        one Humvee remains.
Two men, it seems,
        were made to stay
and carry out
        their comrades' corpses.
There's no big battle.
         You blast them both,
steal the keys
        and start the engine.
The rough tires, spinning,
         spit up water.

The eye's pupil,
        a perfect sun,
implies fine weather,
         but your wipered windshield
shows a shambles:
        shattered storefronts;
trees, trashcans
        and traffic signals
strewn in the street;
        the Starbucks mermaid

downed and dirty;
                          drowned rats, too.
A scenic drive.

                    Soon as you see
that greedy church's
                     great-big cross
and pull over
                on Eighth Avenue,
enclosing clouds
                   eclipse the day.
The wind, Oh God,
                   begins again.

31 *Danse Macabre*

The cataclysm back alive, you lurch
forward against a mother of a squall,
push through the church's front door, shoot the guard
recklessly. Yes, you're wicked mad and all,
but now what? How will you conduct your search?
Is there some big machine from which Canard
will spread The Key throughout the Internet?

Lost and excited, savage, desperate,
you scamper, *splat, splat, splat,* on sopping sneakers
into the now deserted stadium.
You hear there, soft at first, what must be speakers
playing music in some distant room.
A violin is emanating doom
ardently over the infernal thrum
of drum and cello.
                        Following the sound
on down a corridor, you peek around
a corner and, Eureka, you have found
the bastard: he is sitting, statuesque,
grandiose, in a leather swivel chair.
In front of him a silver Macbook Air
is standing open on a glass-top desk.
He is unarmed. He had assumed, no doubt,
his gang of goons had finally snuffed you out,
and nobody could stop him now.

                        You blare,
"Back off the keys or you're a dead man, prick!"

He holds his hands up, chortles and, the thick
Kentucky accent set aside, begins:

"Do you like music? I like violins.

And decadence. This is the *Danse Macabre*,
just the right music for a hurricane.
And Armageddon. Yes, you have a job
to do, but hold on. First let me explain:

I'm not the villain. We, the human race,
are aching for an opportunity
to be as wicked as we want to be.
We need to own our anger, to embrace
our hatreds. If I do us all this favor,
if I share this software, acts of loathing
will cleanse the world. No longer will we waver,
when stung, over the settling of a score.
Each of us, beasts, will shed our moral clothing
and howl! We talk like we are up at arms
and will be, soon.
                    Chaos (my paramour)
is calling to me. All I need to do
is press this button, and my server farms
will spread our native human nastiness
everywhere. We are spoiling to be horrid
to one another. You can feel it. You
will let me press the button, won't you? Yes?"

He reaches, and you shoot him in the forehead.

Nope, he won't be getting up again.

You snatch the plastic drive from the computer
and scan the hallway, hot to fight your way
out of the church, but all the psycho's men,
staring at you, the enemy, the shooter,
just lay their weapons down, as if to say,
The bossman has a bullet in his brain.
There will be no more orders, no more pay.
Why should we bother fighting anymore?
It's over.

        Safely out an exit door,
you drive the Humvee through the hurricane
to Li-ling's place—your place—the address of
peace and release and, now, paternal love.

32 A Wee One

Back in the penthouse, tired of being yourself,
you drop your hoodie on the hardwood floor,
unknot and lose your inundated shoes,
peel off your socks. You feel like one big bruise.
"Honey," you mumble, "Hey, I'm home from war.
I'm not quite dead again." A corner-shelf
presents a bright variety of booze,
but you are too drained even for a bender.

You shamble down the hall and find Li-ling
curled on the long couch in the living room.
Shorts and a loose t-shirt are covering
that tropic zone where what they call "the womb"
immures a future of uncertain gender.
Yawning—though it's only 2 pm
you clamber in around her fetal form.
Outside, the ragged mayhem of the storm;
inside, a wee one being brought to term.
She's got the life, but you are holding them.

Wow, you can almost feel the warm thing squirm.

II. Vision of Destruction

1 Xi Tung

Xi Tung, a poet of the Silver Age
championed for his spirited production
of courtly lyrics on erotic themes,
withdrew into occultism and dreams
after his exile. Late in life, a sage
above affairs and meretricious wit,
he wrote his cryptic *Vision of Destruction*.
Here is the fragment that we have of it:

"I sat one morning on a mountainside
and looked out on a marsh near Lake Dongting
and saw in fog there scenes that signified
the end of man, the end of everything.
When the last cataclysm is at hand,
seven will be the signs:
                              First, from the sea
a monster will arise, a prodigy
that, dead, will breed putrescence. Second, land
animals—leopards, bears—will occupy
the city of all cities, to the north,
still to be built where man has yet to settle.
Third, a hubristic vulture made of metal
will shriek, fall out of the indignant sky
and ram a stone bastion of learning. Fourth. . ."

The page is ripped. The manuscript the Met
is now exhibiting can only whet
a lust for doom: What are the final four
signs of our not existing anymore?

2 The First Omen: Sea-Monster

Todd Wolniak is twelve years old and way,
way bored. He thinks, like, dude, it's just, like, wrong,
like, agony, that every Saturday
his dad goes fishing at the Esplanade
in Battery Park and makes him come along.
It's just not fair. He means, it's just, like, God,
why waste a whole day leaning on the railing,
watching the richies in their sweet boats sailing
round and round? It's been more than a year
since Alfred flooded everything down here.
The place still stinks.
                              His dad does catch an eel
or two, a couple bluefish, maybe flounder
and schlep them home to be the evening meal,
but what's the use? Why spend six hours or more
trying to catch what's at the grocery store?

Suddenly there is revving in a reel.
His father shouts, "feels like a hundred pounder!"
The drag kicks in and ticks until the tight
line breaks. What could have been an epic fight
ends with his father landing on his ass.
His trusty rod, the KastKing Perigee,
goes flying backward up into the park.

Still looking there, just off the Battery,
for the elusive fish, Todd sees a dark
blotch in the slate-gray brine. A pulpous mass
bobs up—a face, it seems, because two eyes,
like dinner plates in coloring and size,
are gaping out of it. Around this head
a whorl of gnarly feelers surfaces,
a mess of herculean grapples, spread

like vermicelli. Todd knows what it is—
a giant squid, and way, way hugely dead.

Oh, he can't wait to tell his friends! How glad
he is that he went fishing with his dad!

3 The Second Omen: Jailbreak

Pelham Parkway, Bronx, at 3 am
is ordinarily not a place of wonder,
but here is "Tweak" Battista, stretched out under
a Ginkgo (his provisional abode),
marveling: is he really seeing them—
two pandas shambling up Boston Road?
Strung out, he questions if his eyes are sound:
Two pandas, and there's no one else around?
If he were not near neighbor to a zoo,
he would dismiss them as hallucination.

He shadows their expansive white behinds
up Bronx Park East toward Pelham Parkway Station.
What, have they made big plans to take the 2
downtown to hit a club near NYU?
Nope, they are turning. They have changed their minds.
They want McDonald's now, it seems. Bamboo
gets old, he figures. Sure, they whiffed a strong
bouquet of sweet, sweet beef all summer long
and now have slipped through their enclosure doors
to stalk New York, reborn as carnivores.

Thank God, he thinks, *I've got no house, no bed
'cause that's where I would be right now instead
of outside seeing. . . Wait. There's something wrong. . .*
Hearing a loud shared purr like that of lovers
off to his right, he pivots and discovers
a pair of big cats dappled with rosettes.
No way these monsters could be someone's pets.
He chuckles (but the joke is mixed with awe):
*They sure are not the first ones in these parts
to go around dressed up in leopard-print!*
While one slinks over and, with massive paw,
roots through a garbage can, the other starts

expressing avaricious bursts of pee
on storefronts: Good & Natural first, then Sprint,
John & Joe's Pizzeria, GNC.

A long train comes, then, and the civic rumble
strikes the beasts as something strange and new
and threatening. While the pandas swiftly bumble
away past Pizza Hut and Planet Fitness,
the other half of the menagerie
lopes left around Tacos El Bronco 2,
tails kinked and bristly. Tweak, unwitting witness
of this the second of the omens, shrugs
and mutters to himself: *Like, who needs drugs?*
Real life is crazier than LSD.

4 Malachi McCann

There is a dark-red village called Hornell
in Steuben County in upstate New York
where self-styled "Führer" Malachi McCann
has built a bunker called "The Citadel"
and crammed the place with hatred, salted pork,
iodine pills, Bibles and bootleg guns.
Oh, he is charismatic—he has drawn
in angry failures, dubbed them "Chosen Ones"
and told them that they must prepare for Hell
in order to survive the End in style.
(They've all been waiting there for quite a while.)

McCann, a highly educated kook,
has read *The Sermon of the Seven Suns*
in Pali and believes the final Buddha
signifies some coming plague or nuke.
He learned the language of the tribe of Judah
and, angry with a new *Good News* translation,
picked Greek up for *The Book of Revelation*
mostly, though he also loves *Baruch*
and *Paul's Apocalypse* and often quotes
what Matthew says about the sheep and goats.
Wow, he has culture, too—the guy can boast
of knowing Wagner's *Götterdämmerung*
auf deutsch—but, listen, here's what matters most:

he reads Mandarin and adores Xi Tung
and owns, complete, *The Vision of Destruction*.
His manuscript is no torn reproduction
but dates to the Eleventh Century.
(All seven signs are in it, all the knowledge
that matters.)

When, on Malachi's TV,
the late news features, first, this long-haired kid
posing, all smiles, beside a big dead squid,
then snow leopards and pandas from the Zoo
digging through trashcans up near Lehman College,
he recognizes omens one and two
have been fulfilled in order.
                                    Taking down
The Vision of Destruction from a shelf,
he mutters, ominously, to himself:
"Looks like it's time for us to go to town."

5 Savannah

You, Zach Berzinski, spy, assassin, bad
mother, for all of your testosterone,
have sworn off violence and become a dad.
That's right: all day you have been home alone
with your insatiate baby girl Savannah.
You have fed her bottle after bottle,
read the warning signs (the squirm, the glottal
spasm) and cringed beneath the burping pad.
Yes, you have even started her on Gerber
Carrot Sweet Potato Pea Banana,
wiped her face and washed a plastic bib.
It's time at last to put the li'l disturber
of other people's slumber in her crib.
Nite-nite.
               The controversial Dr. Ferber
says you should leave her in the nursery,
though she is bellowing like mad, for three
whole minutes, so that she can "cry it out"
and learn to sleep without you. Here you go:
you shut the door behind you.
                              O the slow
hand on your watch-face! O paternal doubt!
When her displeasure rises to a shriek,
you break and rush to soothe her. (You are weak.)

. . . . .

You start from sleep hours later—there are keys
jingling at the door. A TV screen
is all the light left in the living room.
You hear what must be Doc Li-ling Levine
returning, high heels emanating doom.
Entering like a fresh, Siberian breeze,

she finds you lying, drool-soaked, on the couch,
Savannah in your arms.
                        The Met Museum
has put your wife in charge of a Chinese
handscroll exhibit in the Asian Wing.
Before this extra burden, she could be, um,
touchy, but she has been a downright grouch
for weeks now, finding fault with everything
you do and say.
                        What can you say? You told her
you would, in one night, Ferberize the baby,
and here's the baby sleeping on your shoulder.
Flushed with unsuccess, you mutter,
                                "Maybe
our girl is too young yet? Her little throat
gets all scratched up. I mean, it feels like violence,
torture, to leave her screaming."
                                "What it is
is necessary."
                        Since you don't agree,
you turn the volume up with the remote
and kill what would have been an angry silence.

New York One is showing images
of something monstrous, something out of myth
dragged from the water at the Battery.
A bottle-blonde and botoxed talking head
reports the lifeless squid was pregnant with
hundreds of darling larvae, each one dead.
A story titled "Jailbreak from the Zoo!"
comes next—a pair of chubby panda bears
voguing for photos on a set of stairs;
leopards at large on Bronxwood Avenue.

The awkwardness between the two of you
uncoiling, Li-ling says,

"It's strange, you know,
the way things go. At work today I hung
my version of a fragment by Xi Tung,
The Vision of Destruction, for the show.
I gave the text in English word for word:

First will emerge a vast, dead sea-beast, 'fecund'
(he specifies) 'with putrefaction.' Second,
'wild things will run amok' through an immense
metropolis. (By some coincidence
these omens have occurred in order.) Third
should be some sort of 'metal carrion bird'
hitting a wall—but then the text is ripped.
To learn the last four of the seven signs,
we'd need that bit of missing manuscript
but. . .
             kismet, curses, nemesis, life-lines,
what nonsense! Nothing, what a mind 'divines'
is nothing. All we do is stitch together
likelihoods out of has-been happenings.
Accidents can't be forecast like the weather.
Sorry, but there's no 'plan' that rules the things
we humans chance to do."
                              With that, Savannah
(a chick in that most masculine of nests
atop your pecs) starts crying for the manna
Li-ling is storing in her swollen breasts.

6 The Third Omen: Birdstrike

The night is calm and cloudless, and the hour,
very late. The setting: Teterboro
Airport in Jersey. Timothy McGower
has pulled his new G6 out of a hanger.
(He has received approval from the Tower.)
He doesn't want to be around tomorrow
and have to hide from his investors' anger
once they discover their accounts are drained.
Six months ago he secretly obtained
his pilot's license in anticipation
of this covert escape, and, look, the weather
could not be better.
              What's his destination?
Cuba, which has no extradition treaty
with the United States. His teenaged sweetie
Krystal Dijon (the choicest of his blondes)
is waiting there already. A chamois leather
tote containing sheaves of bearer-bonds
totaling 15 billion, all together,
is safe (he checks) beside his pilot's chair.

As Timothy accelerates toward take off,
he thinks, *I'm really going to do it—make off*
with all my clients' money and be free
to party. All I had to do was dare.

(O Timothy, hubristic billionaire,
don't be too hasty in your ecstasy:
there is an echelon of geese, revenge, in
the pre-dawn air.)
              They strike the starboard engine
first, then the port, and he will certainly
be crashing. He can see, Oh God, Times Square
(Madame Tussauds, those giant TV screens),

then recognize, Christ Jesus, Bryant Park
(Ginkgos and maples, various lamplit greens),
then everything goes permanently dark.

7 The Last True Incorruptible

Strolling through Bryant Park at 4 am,
eying the homeless in their patchwork coats,
you think,
       "Oh yeah, I used to live like them—
in wretched freedom, desperate and wild."

Why are you out here? Not for sowing oats:
you love your home, your wife, your chubby child.
It's just, the feral part of you, undead,
is restless, and you are a young man yet.

A shriek sounds then and, passing overhead,
its treble heightening, a private jet
swoops down and rams the Library's Main Branch
over your shoulder.
               Not that gorgeous building. . .
You fell asleep once looking at the gilding
set in the ceiling of The Reading Room. . .
Once on a field trip. . .
               While you are in shock,
the backwall crumbles, and an avalanche
of glass and marble hits the gravel walk.
Dust intermingles with the raveling plume
of black smoke heaving toward you.
                  When that odd
"away" sensation leaves you, and you come
around again, you see, close by, a bum
that looks a lot like Michelangelo's God,
but squalid and with even wilder hair.
Gigantic in a yellow bathrobe, he
is brandishing a flower in his hand
while chanting:

"First the creature from the sea
emerged; then others ran amok by land;
third, now, the iron bird has found the air
hostile and crashed at last. I can recall
what is to come; I have foreseen it all."

Firetrucks are pulling up, and first responders
jumping down and running here and there.

"Are you alright?"

       Cough, cough. You're fine. *Cough, cough.*

Then come the cops, just after local news.

After the crash site has been cordoned off,
the wacko in the dirty bathrobe wanders
among the growing crowd of looky-loos,
intoning, like a priest,
              "I can recall
what is to come; I have foreseen it all."

When morning dusk comes seeping over Queens,
mixing a hint of day into the dark,
you see some guys in black tac-gear and jeans
move in as one. They grab the crazy man
and muscle him away across the park.
The guy, big, drags his heels as best he can,
while sighing in an acquiescent tone:

"All goes according to the Master Plan."

Whatever fight this is, it isn't yours,
but you just can't butt out. Your basso roars,

"Hey there, you bastards, leave that guy alone!"

8 Out of Retirement

On the Great Lawn, a gridiron
                                game begins.
Two from their team
                        turn and rush you,
aspiring sackers.
                    Spoil-sport, you,
rather than running,
                        ready yourself,
then greet, with your foot,
                                the first one's groin.
Kicked where it counts,
                            he, coughing, falls.
Your knuckles welcome
                        the next one's nose.
Blond, he gushes
                    blood on bluegrass—
rhinoplasty
            has ruined him.

Closing, now,
                on the crowd of kidnappers,
you roar, dead-pan,
                    in a heroic voice:
"Unhand that man!"
                        The mass of militants
discharges two more
                    chumps as challengers.

It goes like this:
                    while goon number one
runs up to fight you
                        face to face,
the shrewd second one

sneaks round behind you
and hugs you hard.
                    But who needs hands?
Held up, you bring
                    both feet to bear
on the lead attacker's
                    tender patellae.
On his knees now,
                    he is nothing much.
To beat the prick
                    pinning your arms,
you butt backward
                    with the blunt rear
of your concrete cranium.
                    Cast loose, you swivel
and bury his bulk
                    in body-blows.

Wild, then, you bellow,
                    "Which of you wimps
is next to be maimed?"
                    The remaining mooks
fear you and flee
                    toward 41st Street,
abandoning the big,
                    bathrobe-wearing
kook they had kidnapped.

                    You inquire, panting,
"What was the deal?
                    Why'd they want you?"
Each iris infinite
                    as outer space,
he answers crazy:
                    "Because what's coming
flickers like flashbacks

in my frenzied brain.
I saw the squid,
                    the escaped animals
years before yesterday,
                        and you way back
and this very evening,
                            when the vulture of iron
met the wall.
                I remember it all:
Six certain signs,
                    and the seventh is I,
Orin, oracle
                of Armageddon."

His whirling verbiage
                        washes over you,
and nothing sticks.
                    You need a scholar.

Your tart retort
                to his tangled spiel
is "That sounds brainy.
                    Bud, you'd better
come home with me
                    and meet my wife.
You can throw weird words
                        at one another."

9 The Houseguest

Your new friend muttering, "I can recall
what is to come; I have foreseen it all,"
you make your way downtown and, minutes later,
reach your building. Once the elevator
whisks you and Orin to the seventh floor,
you turn the key in your apartment door.
What's up at home?
                While padding down the hall,
you hear a catastrophic caterwaul,
and there's your wife in sweatpants dandling
your angry child and humming *Clair de Lune*.
She stops; she stares.
             You say, "Um, this is Orin.
He says the human race and everything
is going to be turned to ashes soon.
He's kind of homeless, so I brought him here
to talk it over."
           Flustered by the foreign
presence in her living room, Li-ling
takes you aside and hisses in your ear:
"How could you drag this man in without warning
to shoot the shit at seven in the morning?
Are you insane?"
          You whisper back: "Get off it,
honey. There's trouble coming. What I'm trying
to tell you is this guy's, like, some big prophet.
He knew about the monster from the water
and beasts by land. He knew just now, I swear,
a plane would crash. We need to find somewhere
for him to hide out. I don't want him dying."

Meanwhile, attentive to the sound of crying,
Orin has shambled over to your daughter

and touched her forehead with his filthy palm.
Instantly she is mum. A strange, new calm
descends on her. Her little fists relax.
She sleeps. She sleeps! You pick your darling up
and carry her into the nursery.

A short while later, after you have lent
the guy a T-shirt and a pair of slacks,
served blintzes and refilled his coffee cup,
your wife asks how it is that he can see
futurity and why the scenes his eyes
receive resemble to a great extent
the signs in Xi Tung's poem.
                              He replies,
"Let me explain: I am Xi Tung reborn,
the seventeenth and final avatar.
I know that poem well—it is my own."

She tests him with, "because our copy's torn,
you tell us what the last four omens are."

He shrugs and thunders in a lordly tone:

"... *Fourth, balance will be lost; the proud will totter*
and fall; creation, as if giving birth,
will groan and open, and the blood of earth
will taint the surface of the sterile sea.
Fifth, then, the disparate elements forgetting
the old taboos, there will be fire in water—
an ominous impossibility.
Sixth, then, the sun, on rising in the morning,
will shine blood-red and still be red at noon,
still red at dusk and still red at its setting.
Seventh, when the Untainted One, the last
true Incorruptible, whose voice of warning

has called the signs and told of ruin soon,
is murdered, an exasperated blast
will echo through the New Land, echo through
the Old, pronouncing on the race of men.
There will be nothing anyone can do
but serve as carrion to vultures then.

There ends the poem; there ends all human life.
The thugs who tried to spirit me away
are keen to kill me when the time is right
to wipe out all we are. You and your wife
were fated centuries ago to fight
against them. That's as far as I can say."

You press him, "Me? Li-ling? Why us? Why us?,"
but that's another thing he won't discuss.

10 Pier Thirty-One

Malachi McCann is sick of hating
us people for the vapid way we spend
our stupid lifetimes. He is sick of waiting
for the inevitable apocalypse.
He frankly doesn't care if he survives
or dies. He simply wants the world to end.
After ten years of shrugs and smirks and taunts
from morons living heedless little lives,
he wholly needs our race to come to grips
with being good and dead. Oh yeah, he wants
to teach us all we should have been afraid.

So he and his Catastrophe Brigade
have moved downstate, where he has rented out
a warehouse on the old Pier Thirty-One
to serve as his Manhattan garrison.
When he got notice that at 5 am
a private jet had crashed in Bryant Park,
he smiled and knew that there could be no doubt—
the omens in the poem were coming true.

He roused a squad of men and ordered them
to march out under cover of the dark
and search the crash site for a person who,
distinctive in eccentric dress and style,
might be the seer Xi Tung mentions.
                                                        Well,
where are they? They've been gone for quite a while.
How could their first small job have gone to Hell?

The dawn is brisk, and joggers, briskly paced,
are everywhere. Seagulls are in the air.

While he is looking at the crosstown column
of black smoke curling from the crash, a pair
of cabs pulls up. Six men get out: two solemn;
four limping, miserable and bloody-faced.
The first two soldiers (the uninjured ones)
stop and salute. The rest just groan and bleed.

"What happened?"
                    "Though we found the man you need
and seized him, we encountered much resistance."

"How many were there?"
                    "Just one nasty guy,
a real brute, sir. We should have brought our guns."

A furrowed scowl, a disappointed sigh,
and Malachi says:
                    "Dammit!
                    Well, at least
we now are certain of the seer's existence.
The odds have cinched; the pressure has increased.
We need the one who sees, not just to see
the other omens for us, but to die—
his death will mean the end of this accursed
race of dismissive dopes. The Chinese text
predicts a major earthquake will be next.
If I am right (and I am right), then we
will find him where the damage is the worst."

11 Yes or No

Orin the seer is snoring on your floor.
"That is where I prefer to sleep," he said.
Li-ling went "just to lie down on the bed"
(which means "to nap") a good half-hour ago.
Even Savannah has been sleeping for,
my God, like three hours straight.
                                Yep, you alone
are up and asking questions: Yes or No,
can prophets really scope what is to come?
How does it work? One gets "into the zone"
and views, like in a film, some future scene?
What would these clips of vision issue from?
From God? From Time? What would that even mean?
And who decides who gets to prophecy?
Better the gift come to a homeless guy
than some investor.
                        Anyways, you'll stake
your life, for Li-ling's and the baby's sake,
on his abilities. You'll see this through,
trusting that he's inspired.
                                As if on cue,
the Visionary snorts himself awake
and, all eyes, says, "Earth's entrails will divide!
I see a broken ballpark in the Bronx.
I hear the highways splintering and honks
and crashes everywhere. Soon, soon, the fourth
omen will be fulfilled, and you, my guide,
must take me to its heart. We're heading north!"

. . . . .

How could you not be pissed, since, all the way
up Adam Clayton Powell Boulevard
and over the Macombs Dam (swinging) Bridge,

you, chump, have had the painful privilege
of being an insane man's bodyguard?
The dude would not, for all that you could say,
quit hanging out the window like a dog
and bellowing his epic catalog
of omens prophesying Kingdom Come.
Five times you had to reach across and grab
his belt and yank him back into the cab.

Now that you are across the Harlem River
and coming up on Yankee Stadium,
however, he is silent. What's the matter?
The freak's just sitting there, all furrowed brow,
all sweat and dread. And then he bellows, "Now!"

Your guts jump, and the asphalt starts to shiver.
A housing project shimmies. Windows shatter.

12 The Fourth Omen: Earthquake

At 6:13 pm a seismographic
squiggle of Everest-like amplitude
pronounces, *Woe to Highbridge, Bronx*! The chthonic
throes only escalate. Earth comes unglued.
Land breakers shattering the blacktop, traffic
from Harlem River Drive to the Taconic
honks, swerves and piles up ugly. The tectonic
ecstasy fans out, echoing, downtown.
New York, your day of reckoning has come.

The epicenter, Yankee Stadium,
is dust. All fifty-six exclusive suites
have crumpled, and the most expensive seats
(the ones behind home plate) have tumbled down
into the dugouts. (Seems there was a curse.)

The waves themselves are bad enough but worse
what they deposit in their wake: the soil
pitching and lurching under ranks on ranks
of power poles, the lines rip loose and spark;
then the entire metropolis goes dark.

But what may prove the worst is: storage tanks
containing flammable transformer oil
rupture and glaze the East and Hudson Rivers.
Con Ed, the corporation that delivers
the light of life to Lady Liberty
and everything, had better make a quick
recovery and skim that rainbow slick,
or else, or else. . .we'll have to wait and see.

13 The Rumble in the Rubble

Your buddy Orin,
                the unerring orator
of Armageddon,
                has gone and gotten
atop a raised,
                rebar-encrusted
concrete shard
                and is shouting shaming
words at the world:

                "Woe to all you
heedless humans!
                You hoped to rule
earth forever.
                Your arrogant faith
soon will, surprise!,
                be proven foolish
when the time arrives
                for your total extinction!"

So the guy yawps
                to your ears only
over and over
                for an hour or so.
You try both to tug
                and talk him down
but give up soon
                and gaze at the gritty
billows hovering
                above the debris.

The murk dispersing,
                you make out militants

with Sig Sauer
        assault rifles
moving among
        mounds of concrete.
Whose army are they?
        Under whose orders?
What's their objective?

        To judge from gestures,
the grizzle-bearded
        guy out front
in urban fatigues
        urging them onward
must be in command.
        Their movements are centered
on your tactless companion
        who, tall atop
a peak projecting
        like a preacher's pulpit,
is holding forth.
        They are hunting him.
Rifle rounds
        could already have killed him.
It seems they want him
        safely seized.

Glad you strapped on
        your Glock again,
you draw down, loose lead,
        leap for cover
behind a bank
        of backstop bleachers.
Some grunts repay you
        potshot for potshot.
The gunplay might well
        have gone on a while,

but their sergeant orders,
                    "Cease and desist!
A random ricochet
                could ruin the one
we need alive
          a little longer!"

Spurred by these words,
                  you sprint and spring
onto the slab
           where the soothsayer
is still hollering.
                You hug him, hold him.
The guy going,
           "God won't do it,
but the Weird will,"
              you walk together,
with your arms around him,
                   over the rubble.
The Word says Christ
              crossed the water
on foot like magic.
              Well, man, you make it
a quarter mile
           across cracked concrete
before your foes
            figure they'd better
try tackling
          their target somehow.

When they start circling you,
                  cinching you
in a ring of men,
           you wrap your right arm
around the prophet
            and pop off shots

with your left. Just look at them:
                              leaping, dancing.
Hapless bastards
                    can't blast you back!

That's how it happens—
                              you hugging Orin,
them trying to trap you
                              and retreating shot at
till you carjack
                    a Cabriolet
and drive off downtown
                              through doomed everything.
The seer falls
          asleep beside you.

14 Chip Clark

For all his urban-militant apparel,
Chip Clark has always played the chump in battle—
a runner from the shit, a rotten shooter,
even a pee-er. Well, he chose today
to prove himself: he fixed his rifle barrel
on a surprised delivery-guy astraddle
a neon-orange Vespa motor-scooter,
jacked the thing and set out after you
and Orin in your green Cabriolet.
(He hopes to tell great Malachi McCann
the address where the two of you have gone.)

The sun is setting over Cliffside Park,
and twilight feels like something strange and new
and ominous because the grid is down.
Chip goes on motoring, his headlight dark,
behind you. As you make your way downtown,
he witnesses dense shadow in the squares
and at the major intersections flares
waved by policemen to say stop or go.
Safe driving is, it seems, the thing to do.
Tonight New York, for once, is going slow,
and Chip just goes on creeping with you through
obscurity, your loyal shade, your wraith.
He snickers when you park on 28th.

15 The Talk

Home after violence and a long, dark drive,
you find lit candles on the countertop
and Li-ling at the table. In her lap
your girl, despite a cozy stocking cap
and matching cozy onesie, just won't stop
bellowing like it's Hell to be alive.
So once again your friend, his fingertips
electric with some sedative mystique,
touches her, soothes her. She emits a coo,
yawns and is off to Bye-Bye-Land, and you
remove her. Now the three adults can speak
at ease of imminent apocalypse.

After you chat awhile about the quake
and all, your wife (who can be hard to take)
starts speechifying:
             "Fate: *Moira* in Greek,
Fatum in Latin, *das Shicksal* in German.
Until this morning I was disinclined
to give my credence to foregone events.
But now there's Orin. I have changed my mind.
It seems an outside force does predetermine
some earthly happenings. Just think: four omens
have been fulfilled in order. Who can quibble
with that preponderance of evidence?
Consider history. I mean, the Romans
had books they thought were written by a Sibyl,
a prophetess who told the world of men
when, say, they ought to sacrifice. . ."
                    That's when
you interrupt:
           "Honey, for Heaven's sake,
no way we'll settle things as deep as fate
tonight. I know, though, that our times feel late,

and what's approaching has the power to shake
creation. Still, not all events are fated.
Maybe there's wiggle-room. The only way
to block the end, I figure, is to keep
Orin alive. He has to die, he said,
for our whole race to be exterminated.
We'll keep him safe."
                      There's nothing more to say.
The day has drained you all. You go to sleep,
you and Li-ling on a four-poster bed,
Orin recumbent on the hardwood floor.

. . . . .

Waking, you hear a resonant voice proclaim:
"Behold, all round, the wicked liquid flame!"
But, by the time you get some boxers on
and run into the living room, he's gone.
Cussing, you dash, half-naked, out the door.

16 Faster, Faster!

A mad dash to the lobby, flight by flight,
and you have just begun to pant, to sweat.
Out on the street the darkest New York night
for years is going on. Star-clusters lend
a rural twinkling, and a bum has set
the contents of a garbage-can alight,
and you can just discern your giant friend
the Visionary vanishing. A pack
of thugs is dragging him into a black
Humvee. They squeal away past Chelsea Park.

How can you catch them now? No cabs in sight,
you rip a Citi Bike out of its base
and take off after taillights through the dark
streets southward. Pumping at an all-out pace,
your naked soles go raw by 20th.
By 16th you are almost out of breath,
but on you pedal, butt high off the seat,
and then at last the twin red lights start burning,
burning. The boxy beast is slowing, turning
west toward the Hudson on 11th Street.

The taillights darken at the riverside.
You ditch the bike and dash on bloody feet
just near enough to see thugs drag the seer
into a creaking warehouse on a pier.
Though in your underwear, you have your pride
to urge you onward. You can't let your friend
be murdered, you can't let the known world end.

17 One Against Hundreds

Much has happened:
                    mere minutes after
stalking a sentry,
                    strangling him,
and filching his fancy,
                    fully-auto
assault-rifle,
                    mere seconds after
scaling the wall
                    and squeezing through
a gap of rot
                    where the roof begins,
you, bare-naked
                    but for your boxers,
stand, raw-footed,
                    with rats on a rafter,
surveying the scene.
                    You see beaucoup
goons with rifles
                    ranged around
a tiki torch.

        In the tentative light
their grizzle-bearded
                    boss is bellowing
at your friend Orin,
                    "The fifth sign, the fire
that thrives on water—
                    where and when
and how will it start?"
                    Stubborn in the face
of ornery authority,
                    Orin answers:

"Soon enough you
           will see for yourself
just what I witness,
           though you won't want
to see it then."
           Incensed by this,
the guy winds up
           and wallops Orin's
left ear hard.
           Your huge friend staggers,
takes a knee.

           Torn between
red rage demanding
           an immediate rampage
and neutral prudence
           nagging, outnumbered,
you will be quickly
           killed while killing,
you wince and worry:
           what should you do?

18 The Fifth Omen: Fire on the Water

Claire Custer, born and bred in Rocky Ridge,
Utah, has ridden her beglittered bike
through Chinatown and up the Brooklyn Bridge.
Once at the top, she lights a Lucky Strike
(A British friend has given her the pack.)
and leans her forearms on the iron railing.

Why is she blissful, why at peace, in spite
of shattered freeways and the power failing?
Because the big night sky, at last, is back.
(It's easy to forget how very black
space is when one is reveling in the gaudy
ecstasy of Manhattan every night.)

She squints awhile, and scattered points of light
gather themselves, for her, into Orion,
the skewed head and interminable body
of Draco, either Bear, the Swan, the Lyre,
even the Dolphin and the Lesser Lion.

When her cigarette is almost done,
she drops the still-lit butt (a smidge of fire)
over the railing. Time to go to bed.
But holy . . . an eruption has begun
beneath her. There is rumbling on the water,
and orange there. An exhalation hotter
than any earthly breeze has singed the air.
Just look at that! The liquid blaze has spread
so far already up and down the river.
Already flames have found the bars and stores
that line the South Street Seaport.
                              Claire, O Claire,
you new Prometheus, you shy fire-giver,
why have you up and pedaled off instead
of staying to admire this work of yours?

19 *Nox Irae*

A hush like held breath
                    hangs a moment
then, whoa, what's that?
                    A wild whoosh
lights up everything,
                    like a gas-stove's
burner igniting.
                    Boards combust;
the wood warehouse
                    is wearing flames.
The inferno seems
                    something summoned
by brutish magic,
                    your brain's own brimstone
unleashed at last.

                    The unlucky goons
on the outside catch,
                    and the recruits crowded
between them panic,
                    push toward exits.
In the tight chaos,
                    troops, trampled,
are left lying
                    like living kindling.
You see a hundred
                    horrors happen
all at the same time:
                    some, set alight,
dash through weak
                    walls toward water
but find the Hudson
                    hellish as well;

some, bodies strung
>
> with bullet-belts,

are immolated,

>
> ammo exploding;

some, in a scrum,

>
> scramble screaming

desperately toward

>
> the dockside door.

Focus, man, focus.

>
> Finding finally,

in the orange aura,

>
> Orin again,

you run toward him

>
> from rafter to rafter,

drop down barefoot

>
> and, dancing, shout,

"Move it, moron;

>
> make for the door!"

Blasé about

>
> being rescued,

your friend just shrugs,

>
> like, "show me the way."

So you begin,

>
> soles simmering,

to pilot the prophet

>
> through a pandemonium

of flames, curses

>
> and flailing arms.

When you are almost

>
> out the exit

that goddamn guy, though,

>
> the graybeard, grabs

Orin's waist

>
> and won't let go.

Roaring, you raise
                    the rifle-butt
and thunk the bastard's
                      thick head hard.
He falls back, lies there
                    as fire-fodder.
Nite-nite, annoyance.

                  Newborn at last
from a wobbly warehouse
                    like a womb of flame,
you and the seer
                sit, soot-stained,
on the riverbank.
                The roof collapses.

20 The Sixth Omen: Sun Like Blood

The air is so smoke-choked, so thick and gritty,
that an indignant sun has come up blushing
darker than it ever has before
over the Hamptons, Floral Park and Flushing.

All night the fire leapt up into the city;
all night the firemen of the South Street Station
have battled it and still are waging war
at dawn. Yanked snoring from a creaky cot
and told to go and fight the conflagration,
Howard "The Hose" Petrossian has fought
and fought to save the roof of old St. James,
but he is all aches now, and perspiration,
and losing heart.
                    Expert in every law
pertaining to his trade, he feels these flames
are something supernatural, something more
than mere ferocity. He is marooned
(he fears) by hellfire. Claustrophobic awe
has left him gasping, and his back is sore.
His palms, in spite of leather gloves, are raw.
God, won't this brimstone ever just stop burning?

The sun (he thinks) is like an open wound
discharging crimson on Manhattan. Turning,
he says to big Pete Teague beside him, "Bud,
this whole damn day is gonna look like blood."

21 Roses Are Red

Here you are, in your much-smutched underwear,
limping on raw feet north through Greenwich Village,
Orin beside you. Everywhere the blare
of sirens, sirens. Ash is in the air,
and anarchy: ghosts impudently pillage
phones, laptops, cameras and stereos
from a defenseless electronics store;
dark fashionistas raid boutiques for clothes—
a dozen shattered windows and for blocks
mannequins stripped to their designer socks.
Oh, let it go. You don't care anymore.
For all your race is covetous and wrong,
you have at least saved Orin.
                            When the long
night dies at last and sunrise hits Manhattan,
light, as if passing through a crimson filter,
ruddies the gloom. Jays tweet a bloody matin.
What darkroom is this? What will day expose?
Human indifference's dragon-spawn?
The blooming of a catastrophic rose?

You limp on, cussing, as the world, off-kilter,
wobbles toward some uncertain denouement.
Orin just keeps on grinning, since he *knows*.
To him the epic outcome is foregone.

22 The Final Morning?

Victorious, you should return in glory,
but more pain greets you when you reach your street—
you have to halt up to the seventh story
on blistered agony, on weeping feet.

Li-ling freaks out about how bad you look.
Savannah won't stop raising Cain—it seems
she gets that something's wrong. Your buddy Orin
takes her and tucks her in his elbow crook,
and, smiling, she is out at once. Sweet dreams.

After you shower off a layer of ash
and throw your dirty boxers in the trash,
Li-ling breaks out a tube of Neosporin
and rubs it on your incandescent soles
and heels, your arches, in-between your toes.

Dressed in a hotel bathrobe then, whole rolls
of bandages around your feet, you start
to fret about your little girl again.
Dad as you are, whatever happens, when
it happens, you will play a father's part.

You take Savannah, shuffle gingerly
into the nursery and lay her down.
Outside the picture window you can see
a superstorm of soot all over town.
The sun is blood; the rivers are ablaze.
No morning ever seemed so ripe for doom.

Li-ling cream-cheeses bagels, and the three
of you get settled in the living room
to have another chat about the end of days.

23 Götterdämmerung

Look out, now—there is trouble south of you.

The sun, still bloody hours after dawn,
has found a shape on Seventh Avenue,
the ragged shape of Malachi McCann,
alive. He scarcely can remember how.
There was a blast, a fight, and when his torrid
Valhalla fell into the Hudson River,
he went down, too, but swam ashore and now,
demoniac with flame-scarred brows and forehead,
is an Avenger burning to deliver
creation from the plague of humankind.
So many parasitic upright vermin!
Oh yes, he has to wipe us out, or else he
will die for nothing.
           Past 14th, in Chelsea,
pain drives him even further from his mind.
Brünnhilde is intoning Wagner's German
ardently, and he starts to hum the part
that goes *helles Feuer das Herz mir erfaßt*
("The fire of Hell has now possessed my heart").

A bit more violence, that is for the best,
and human folly will be in the past;
A bit more violence, and the world will rest.

24 On the Advice of Dr. Ferber

The little chat on fate winds down round noon.
The takeaway: a staunch resolve to keep
your friend the prophet safe, no matter what.

When a barrage of devilishly deep
shrieks issues from your daughter's plush cocoon,
and Orin goes to soothe the child again,
Li-ling insists she loves Savannah, but
"the child must learn to cry herself to sleep."
You and the prophet, "wishy-washy men,"
must, under no conditions, comfort her.

Oh God, she has removed the infant, shut
the door behind her and returned, arms crossed.
The same old hopes and same old doubts recur:
Will your exasperating girl exhaust
her little lungs? Will she give in at last?
One painful minute, two, then three, have passed,
three ages, and you still can hear Savannah.
(They probably can hear her in Montana.)

"Knock, knock!" Just when you can no longer stifle
your empathy, and tears begin to fall,
you hear a voice shout "Knock, knock!" from the hall
outside of the apartment. "Knock, knock, knock!"
Then, what must be an automatic rifle
rips up the oak veneer, blows out the lock.
That bastard from before, but now with skin
blistered and lizardlike, comes charging in.

25 He, a Horror

He, a horror
　　　　　in half-burnt boots,
strides down the front hall,
　　　　　　　　　stops and stands there
shooting up
　　　　　your open-plan home.
Your lithe wife leaps
　　　　　　　　for the lino and slides
behind the marble
　　　　　　　mid-kitchen island.
You hug the prophet,
　　　　　　　hold him to you
as sacrosanctly
　　　　　　　as a secret-service
agent would press
　　　　　　　his precious president.
You heave, then, bring
　　　　　　　your bulk to bear.
The tackle works:
　　　　　　　two in tandem
hit the hardwood,
　　　　　　　hide together
safely behind
　　　　　　the sectional sofa.

The big gun roams
　　　　　　　at random, riddles
drop-ceiling, drywall,
　　　　　　　drapes and window.
Rat-a-tat-crash,
　　　　　　　and you cringe to hear
your banshee baby
　　　　　　　in the background shrieking.

Your mind fractures.
                    Too many rival
roles to perform:
                    father, friend,
husband. Whom
                    should you help out first?

Orin answers,
                    ends your indecision,
by slipping from your grip,
                              standing and stating,
"What must be done
                    is mine in memory.
This ending is
                    the only answer."
The intruder's fateful
                         trigger-finger
coming down,
              you dive desperately—
the human race
                hangs in the balance.

26 Your Better Half

Shoulder shot,
                you shudder, plummet.
A kilim catches you,
                   but you can't fight on.
Useless malingerer,
                you must merely
gape as he trains
            his gun again
on your friend the seer,
                the Seventh Sign.
You writhe there, waiting
                  for one momentous
round to erase
            the race of man,
undo creation.
            Your darling daughter
won't stop wailing.

            Here's where your wife
makes her move:
            she mounts the grizzled
monster from the rear
              and, right radius
tight up under
            his tender throat,
starts pulling,
            strangling the pulmonary
essence out of him.
            Aspirating,
he bucks bull-like,
              backs up, rams her
against the wall,
            the wood-block prints.

Your better half
            just holds on harder,
wrings his neck,
            while knocking knick-knacks
off the top
            of the rattan end table.

And then the creature
            quits resisting.

27 A Man and His Dog

What Malachi McCann perceives, while dying,
is not lost love or flickers from his youth
but foreign imagery that glows like truth,
and he relaxes.
                             In his eyes, two scrying
crystals, there is a man, a failed believer,
who keeps a junkyard in a desert place.
The man is coughing, and his black retriever
has jumped up on the bed to lick his face.
The dog (he named it "Bud") showed up one day
and watched the man and begged, a curious stray,
till scraps left out developed into trust,
and mutual touch became a sort of love.

Why here? Why them? What are they symbols of?
Who knows? But now the junkyard man has died
and, after three days lying by his side,
Bud wanders off into the desert dust.

The villain, choking, sees this, scene by scene,
dies with it in his eyes. What does it mean,
except that even lost souls, in the end,
deserve the love of Someone? Call Him "Man's Best Friend."

28 Nite-Nite

Cut off, the creep
                can't keep standing.
Gone to his knees,
                he is gasping, gasping
until at last
              life has left him.
He falls face-forward,
                 followed by her,
your wife, the savior.
                Silence reigns.

Yes, that grumpy
                girl of yours,
Savannah, has screamed
                 herself to sleep
for the first time ever,
                Ferberized now.

29 The Pieces

Events blur by a while: it seems Li-ling
has helped you to the lobby, brought her car
around and whisked you to a packed ER;
forceps have pulled a bullet out of you;
kind hands have wrapped bandages round your feet
and tied your forearm in a shoulder-sling.
Six weeks, and you will be as good as new.

Now you are swaying on your own home street
under the spell of some sweet opiate.
Orin the Visionary Voice of Doom
had kindly stayed behind to baby-sit.
You find your darling daughter sleeping more
tranquilly than she ever has before,
and you, too, ache to go lie down. . .
        but hold it—
there is a carcass in your living room.
The walking wounded, you can't deal with it.
Even before you ask, your friend has rolled it
up in the kilim, dragged it out the door.
The power is out, and so no elevator.
You watch him push the bundle, floor by floor,
down to the loading dock, out to the alley.

Goodbye to what's-his-face, obsessive hater
of his own humankind. That's one more task
completed. Now there's nothing left to do
but ponder what has happened.
        Stoned, you ask
Orin if he foresaw the grand finale—
that creep, his rifle, Li-ling strangling him.

He says, "I saw his gun, my chest. I knew
I had to face him. All the rest was dim.

133

No, I was just a human medium.
I glimpsed mere moments of a Master Plan
but never knew it Alpha to Omega.

Henceforth I will be happy to be mum
about the future. What will come will come.
I want to be an ordinary man
who sleeps the night through, stops at the bodega
for coffee in the morning, works eight hours
and hits the bars. I want to be as blind
to fate as all the rest of humankind.
Selflessness—that's what comes from special powers."

Back up in the apartment, Orin gives
your sleeping child a parting coochy-coo.
His handshake with Li-ling turns to a hug.
When she inquires, "What are you going to do—
you know—out there?," he answers with a shrug,
then says, "what every person does who lives
without a calling and without a goal:
breathe without knowing what I'm breathing for."

With that, he walks out through your riddled door
not like a man who lost something, but one
whose eagerness for life has just begun.
His future will be, mostly, under his control.

30 At the Grave of Xi Tung

Halfway around the world a cloudless night
is covering the slopes of Mount Laojun
and Xi Tung's cracked gravestone, a landmark site
visited only by the fickle moon.
Why didn't young hands tend this ancestor?
The rugged plot is overgrown with burr
and thistle. Is his spirit even there?
Was he condemned to be a restless ghost?

For centuries the genius who forecast
far-away signs and modern-day disasters
traveled, it seems, from foreign host to host.
His prescient message was, *Beware, Beware.*
But what was destined now is in the past.

Out in the cold air, through a crust of snow,
a purple jonquil blooms, as if the master's
roving spirit has come home at last.

The future is our own, for all we know.

31 All Grown Up

Li-Ling is in the kitchen with a broom
sweeping up remnants of the late affair
in which she squeezed the life out of a crazy
killer and saved the human race. You, hazy
on the sofa in the living room,
are lying on your right side, your good shoulder,
watching Savannah in her bouncy-chair.

Her little legs keep pushing at the tile
they soon enough will toddle on. You smile.
How much you want your girl, as she gets older,
to drink in, as if from a sippy cup,
happiness from the passing of her days.

But you are whom this novel had to raise;
you are the one who has at last grown up.

About The Author

AARON POOCHIGIAN earned a PhD in Classics from the University of Minnesota and an MFA in Poetry from Columbia University. His thriller-in-verse, *Mr. Either/Or*, was released by Etruscan Press in the fall of 2017. A recipient of an NEA Grant in translation, he has published translations with Penguin Classics and W. W. Norton. His latest book *American Divine*, the winner of the Richard Wilbur Award, came out in 2021. His other poetry collections are *Manhattanite* (Able Muse Press, 2017), winner of the 2016 Able Muse Book Award, and *The Cosmic Purr* (Able Muse Press, 2012). His work has appeared in such publications as *Best American Poetry*, *The Paris Review* and *POETRY*.

Books from Etruscan Press

Etruscan Press Is Proud of Support Received From

Wilkes University

Youngstown State University

Ohio Arts Council

The Stephen & Jeryl Oristaglio Foundation

Community of Literary Magazines and Presses

National Endowment for the Arts

Drs. Barbara Brothers & Gratia Murphy Endowment

The Thendara Foundation

Founded in 2001 with a generous grant from the Oristaglio Foundation, Etruscan Press is a nonprofit cooperative of poets and writers working to produce and promote books that nurture the dialogue among genres, achieve a distinctive voice, and reshape the literary and cultural histories of which we are a part.

etruscan press

www.etruscanpress.org

Etruscan Press books may be ordered from

Consortium Book Sales and Distribution
800.283.3572
www.cbsd.com

Etruscan Press is a $501(c)(3)$ nonprofit organization.
Contributions to Etruscan Press are tax deductible
as allowed under applicable law.
For more information, a prospectus,
or to order one of our titles,
contact us at books@etruscanpress.org.